W9-COR-553

Fergus
to the Rescue

For Karin

First published in 2002 in Great Britain by
Piccadilly Press Ltd, London
www.piccadillypress.co.uk

Text and illustrations copyright © Tony Maddox 2002

This 2010 edition published by Sandy Creek by arrangement with Piccadilly Press

All rights reserved. No part of this publication may be reproduced,
stored in a retrieval system, or transmitted in any form or by any means
electronic, mechanical, photocopying, recording or otherwise,
without prior written permission from the publisher.

Sandy Creek
122 Fifth Avenue
New York, NY 10011

ISBN: 978 1 4351 2329 8

1 3 5 7 9 10 8 6 4 2

Printed and bound in China

Fergus
to the Rescue

Tony Maddox

Sandy Creek

Summer was almost over.
Everyone had been helping load the hay.
Farmer Bob looked up at the dark clouds,
"Better hurry!" he said.
"Looks like we're in for a storm."

When the hay was safely stored,
Fergus found a comfortable spot in the barn
and settled down to sleep.
He was much too tired to go back to his dog house.

That night the storm came
and the rain poured down.
Fergus was glad he was
warm and safe in the barn.

The next morning Fergus woke up to find the barn surrounded by water.
Farmer Bob drove up and shouted,
"Take care of the animals, Fergus!
I'll go and see what has happened!"

Fergus rounded up the animals and hurried them into the barn.

He counted everyone.
"One cow ... two ducks ... three pigs and four ...!"
WHERE WERE THE HENS?

Fergus ran outside and
called loudly . . .

He waded out towards the sound until he saw the henhouse roof sticking up out of the water. And there were the hens perched on top. They were shivering from the cold and looked very scared.

"Cluck cluck cluck!" they called.

The water was now too deep for Fergus to reach them. He had to find something that would float. He rushed back to the barn. "Woof woof woof!"
Fergus told the animals of his plan to rescue the hens.
They all agreed to help.

All they could find was a rusty bucket,

They carried them to the water's edge

some cooking pots and an old tin bath.

and tied them together with rope.

When the makeshift boat was ready, Fergus clambered aboard. With the ducks paddling, he set off to rescue the hens.

When the hens saw Fergus, they jumped up and down and flapped their wings. "We're here, Fergus! We're here!" they clucked excitedly.

In no time at all, the hens were safely aboard Fergus's strange boat. On the way back, they also rescued a family of field mice, two very wet rabbits and a squirrel.

Farmer Bob was there to
meet them.
"The river overflowed,"
he explained.
"It's better now, so the farmyard
will soon be back to normal."

They went back to the farmhouse to dry off and make buttered toast in front of the glowing fire. Farmer Bob's wife brought them hot cider.

"I think you've all earned it!" she said.